G is for Gree

Spike and Chip came out of the house carrying the box of gold. Gram Hathaway followed them onto the porch.

"Thanks, Mrs. Hathaway," Spike said. "Do you really think your friends will help us?"

Gram Hathaway smiled. "I wouldn't be a bit surprised. I'm going to talk to my banker on Monday morning!"

A yellow cab pulled up. Spike and Chip got in and sped away. Ruth Rose's grandmother went back into the house.

"She's pretty excited," Ruth Rose said.

"I would be, too, if I was gonna get rich," Josh said.

"I don't think she's gonna get rich," Dink said. "I think she's gonna get robbed!"

To Fred and Mary, bestest friends
—R.R.

In memory of Gromere
—J.S.G.

Text copyright © 1999 by Ron Roy
Cover art copyright © 2015 by Stephen Gilpin
Interior illustrations copyright © 1999 by John Steven Gurney

All rights reserved. Published in the United States by Random House Children's Books,
a division of Random House LLC, a Penguin Random House Company, New York.
Originally published in paperback by Random House Children's Books, New York, in 1999.

Random House and the colophon and A to Z Mysteries are registered trademarks
and A Stepping Stone Book and the colophon and the A to Z Mysteries colophon
are trademarks of Random House LLC.

Visit us on the Web!
SteppingStonesBooks.com
randomhousekids.com

Educators and librarians, for a variety of teaching tools, visit us at RHTeachersLibrarians.com

Library of Congress Cataloging-in-Publication Data
Roy, Ron.
The goose's gold / by Ron Roy ; illustrated by John Steven Gurney.
p. cm. — (A to Z mysteries)
"A Stepping Stone book."
Summary: When Ruth Rose and her friends, vacationing in Florida, discover that her grandmother is about to invest in a project to recover sunken treasure, they stumble upon evidence that the entire plan may be a fraud.
ISBN 978-0-679-89078-2 (trade) — ISBN 978-0-679-99078-9 (lib. bdg.) —
ISBN 978-0-307-52905-3 (ebook)
[1. Buried treasure—Fiction. 2. Florida—Fiction. 3. Mystery and detective stories.]
I. Gurney, John, ill. II. Title. III. Series: Roy, Ron. A to Z mysteries.
PZ7.R8139 Go 1999 [Fic]—dc21 98-46152

Printed in the United States of America
44 43 42 41 40 39 38 37 36 35

This book has been officially leveled by using the F&P Text Level Gradient™ Leveling System.

Random House Children's Books supports the First Amendment and celebrates the right to read.

A TO Z Mysteries®

The Goose's Gold

by Ron Roy

illustrated by
John Steven Gurney

A STEPPING STONE BOOK™

Random House New York

Chapter 1

"Hi, Mom, I'm in Florida!" Dink said into the phone. He glanced out the airport's large windows. "I can see palm trees! And it's about 80 degrees!"

Donald David Duncan, known as Dink to his friends, was on winter vacation from school. He, Josh, and Ruth Rose were visiting Ruth Rose's grandmother. She lived on an island called Key West.

Dink's mother told him to have a wonderful time. "And remember your manners!"

Dink grinned into the phone. "What manners? Just joking, Mom! See you in a few days."

Dink hung up the phone. As he bent over to pick up his backpack, he saw a pair of feet in the next booth. They were tan and in sandals. One hairy ankle had a tattoo of an eagle's head.

Dink heard the man's voice. He was whispering, "...then we take the dough and split. They'll never find us!"

Take the dough and split? Was this guy planning a robbery? Dink wondered.

He leaned toward the other booth so he could hear better.

"Those old cookies are loaded," the

man whispered. "We get in and out, then we drown the goose and disappear!"

Dink blinked. Loaded cookies? Drown the goose? What was going on here?

Suddenly, Josh snapped his fingers in front of Dink's face. "Earth to Dink," he said.

"Come on, we have to go find my grandmother," said Ruth Rose.

Dink stepped away from the phone. He peeked into the next booth, but it was empty.

Dink hurried after Josh and Ruth Rose.

"You guys aren't gonna believe what I just heard!" he said. "I think some guy is planning a robbery!"

Josh and Ruth Rose looked at Dink. "Are you kidding?" Ruth Rose asked.

"No, honest!" Dink said.

Dink tried to imitate the way the man had whispered. "He said, 'take the dough and drown the goose!'"

Josh looked at his friend. "That's it?"

Dink nodded. "Well, he also said something about loaded cookies."

"Maybe he said 'bake the dough and brown the goose,'" Ruth Rose said. "Sounds like he was a chef, not a robber."

Suddenly, they heard someone call, "Yoo-hoo, kids. Over here!"

"There she is," Ruth Rose said excitedly. "HI, GRAM!"

The kids hurried over to a smiling woman with white hair.

"Honey, how you've grown!" Ruth Rose's grandmother said. She gave Ruth Rose a hug. "Merry Christmas!"

Ruth Rose blushed. "Thanks, Gram. These are my best friends, Dink and Josh. Guys, this is Gram Hathaway!"

Gram Hathaway was short and tanned. She wore shorts, a purple T-shirt, and a baseball cap—backward!

Gram shook hands with the boys. "I've heard a lot about you two," she said. "Got your bags? Let's go home and have a nice supper."

Ruth Rose's grandmother led them through the exit doors. The evening was hot and humid. Everyone wore shorts and sandals.

"Boy, back home we had a foot of snow!" Josh said. "I can't wait to see the ocean!"

"There's a lovely beach not far from my house," Ruth Rose's gram said. "I think you'll find the water pretty warm for December."

They piled into her small white car. "Buckle up, everyone," she said.

Dink and Josh climbed in the back. Dink almost sat on a pair of in-line skates. "Just dump those on the floor," Gram said.

Josh snuck Dink a look. "Do you skate?" he asked Ruth Rose's grandmother.

She winked at Josh in the rearview mirror. "Only on Tuesdays and Fridays.

The rest of the week I jog or swim!"

A few minutes later, they were zooming along a busy street. Dink watched the tall palm trees as the car whizzed past them. Through rows of neat houses, he caught glimpses of blue sea and nearly white sand.

"Look, a pelican!" Josh cried, pointing out the window.

"You'll see plenty of those here," Gram Hathaway said. "And they aren't afraid of people. I saw one swoop down and snatch a girl's ice cream cone!"

"They better not try that with me!" Josh said.

"Here we are," Gram Hathaway said. She pulled her car into a driveway surrounded by rosebushes.

Dink saw a small pink house with blue shutters. Window boxes were filled with bright flowers. Pots of pink geraniums sat on the front steps.

"You've got an awesome house, Mrs. Hathaway!" Josh said.

She laughed. "Please call me Gram, and thank you!"

The kids followed Gram into a yellow living room. In one corner, a Christmas tree stood on a table.

"Okay, drop your bags and let's eat!"

Gram led Ruth Rose and Josh into her kitchen. "I hope you like fried chicken!"

Dink followed slowly. He couldn't stop thinking about the man on the telephone.

If he was just talking about food, Dink wondered, why was he whispering?

Chapter 2

"I smell cookies," Josh said the next morning.

Dink rolled over and looked at Josh. He was sitting up in bed with his nose in the air.

Dink grinned. "You look like a rabbit, Josh."

"No, I'm serious," Josh said. He

walked over to the window and took a deep whiff. "Yep, it's cookies. With chocolate chips!"

They heard a knock on their bedroom door. "Hurry up, you guys!" Ruth Rose said. "Gram is making breakfast!"

Dink and Josh scrambled into shorts and T-shirts. They did a quick job of washing up, then hurried down the stairs.

Gram Hathaway stood at the stove, spooning pancake batter onto a hot griddle. She was wearing running gear, and her hair was tied in a red bandanna. "Good morning, boys. How'd you sleep?"

"Great," Dink said. "Except Josh snored all night!"

"Ha!" Ruth Rose laughed as she poured orange juice into four glasses. She liked to dress all in one color. Today she was wearing green shorts, a green

T-shirt, and green jelly shoes.

Josh glanced at the stove. "I thought I smelled chocolate chip cookies."

Gram smiled. "What an observant young man! There's a batch in the oven that's almost done."

Josh nudged Dink. "See? I'm an observant young man!"

Gram brought a platter of pancakes to the table. "I'm baking cookies for our company."

"Who's the company, Gram?" Ruth Rose asked.

Her grandmother smiled mysteriously. "It's a surprise. You'll have to wait and see."

While they ate breakfast, Gram told the kids about some of the sights to see on the island.

"Be sure to take a ride on the Old Town Trolley," she said. "It scoots all over town."

"How do we get to the beach?" Josh asked.

"Just walk to the end of my street, then turn right," Gram said. "Two more blocks, and you'll see the water!"

"Can we help you clean up?" Ruth Rose asked.

"I'll clean up after my run," Gram replied. "You kids go have fun, and I'll see you for lunch."

The kids each grabbed a warm cookie, then hurried outside.

Ten minutes later, they were carrying their sneakers and wading in the ocean.

Dink was looking at guys' feet on the beach. He saw plenty of ankle tattoos, but none were eagles.

From the beach, they walked up some steps to a wide concrete pier. There were benches and tables, and vendors selling food and souvenirs. A man was juggling oranges and grape-fruits. Big gray pelicans sat on posts, waiting for tourists to feed them.

"Let's go see those boats," Josh suggested, pointing toward a long wooden dock.

The kids ran along the beach and crossed over to the dock. Dink saw a sign that said WATCH FOR SPLINTERS AND FISHHOOKS! NO BARE FEET!

People were lined up, fishing. One little girl shouted, then pulled up a silver fish the size of Dink's hand.

The kids pulled on their shoes and hiked along the long dock. Boats were nestled in slips on both sides.

Everywhere they looked, people were washing, polishing, or painting their boats.

"I wish I had a sailboat," Josh said as they continued along the dock. "I'd live on it and sail around the world."

"What about me and Dink?" Ruth Rose asked.

"Oh, I'd hire you as my cook," Josh told Ruth Rose. "You could make me cookies and pizza."

He nudged Dink with his hip. "And Dinkus could wash my clothes and make my bed!"

"Yeah, right," Dink said. "And make you walk the plank!"

"Listen! I hear music," Josh said.

A radio stood at the end of the dock next to a man holding a paintbrush. He was painting curly gold letters on the side of a white boat. So far, he'd finished G and O.

Smears of gold speckled the man's tanned fingers. He was short, but the muscles on his arms made him look like a weightlifter.

Another man stood next to him, eating a muffin. He was tall and skinny,

with a blond ponytail. Both men wore tank tops over baggy jeans.

The skinny man nodded at the kids. "Howdy," he said.

"I like your boat," said Josh. "Do you live on it?"

The skinny man turned down the radio. "There're two beds up front," he said. "A kitchen and a bathroom, too."

Dink noticed a yellow rubber dinghy strapped along one side of the boat. Two long fishing poles were lying on the deck.

"Is it a fishing boat?" Dink asked.

The skinny man shook his head. "Naw, we're after treasure. We dive for gold."

"You do?" Josh said. "Cool!"

The man waved his muffin out at the ocean. "There're plenty of sunken ships out there," he said, grinning. "Me and Spike here found one."

The man with the paintbrush gave his friend a sharp look. "Chip, maybe these kids don't want to know our business," he said.

Chip shrugged. "Just bein' neighborly," he said.

Spike went back to his painting.

"Did you find any gold yet?" Josh asked.

Chip looked at Spike.

"Yeah, we got some," Spike said.

"Could we see it?" Ruth Rose asked.

Spike thought for a minute, then handed Chip his paintbrush. "Sure, why not?" he said. "Come aboard and watch your feet."

Spike climbed down some stairs to a little cabin. When he came back up, he had something shiny in his hand.

"These are Spanish coins," Spike told the kids. "Almost four hundred years old."

The kids stared at the gold coins in Spike's hand.

"Pretty neat, huh?" he asked.

The large gold coins gleamed in the sun.

"Awesome!" Josh said.

Chapter 3

The kids thanked Spike and Chip and walked back along the dock.

"I wonder how much those coins are worth," Josh said.

"A lot!" Ruth Rose said.

Josh sighed. "Wouldn't it be cool to dive for treasure?"

"Josh," Dink said, "you need to

know how to use an air tank and everything. They go down deep!"

Across the street, a small orange train was loading up with passengers.

"There's the trolley!" Ruth Rose said. "Let's catch it!"

The kids rushed over. They climbed aboard and sat right behind the driver. When most of the seats were filled, the trolley gave a jolt, then moved down the street.

"Where does the trolley go?" Dink asked the driver.

"We go everywhere, my man!" said the driver. He handed Dink a map. "See those blue circles? Those are my stops.

You can get off at any of them, then hop
back on when I come by again."

The driver stopped the train in front
of a white building with overflowing
flower boxes. The sign in front of the
building read MEL FISHER'S TREASURE
MUSEUM. SEE SPANISH GOLD AND SILVER INSIDE.

"Who's Mel Fisher?" Dink asked the driver.

"Mel Fisher found an old Spanish ship loaded with gold and silver," he said. "Some of what he found is in this museum."

He pointed at the sign. "Why don't you kids hop off and check it out? I'll swing by again in about forty-five minutes."

"All right!" Josh said.

The kids got off the trolley and followed a few of the other sightseers to the museum.

Inside were rows of glass cases. Each case held gleaming gold, silver, or jewelry.

The kids walked around the room staring at the priceless treasures.

After a while, Ruth Rose stopped in front of a picture of Mel Fisher. He was wearing a long gold chain. The real chain was displayed in a glass case below the picture.

"Listen," Ruth Rose said. "'This solid gold chain was made in 1622 and weighs 200 pounds. It is worth more than one million dollars!'"

"Boy, imagine wearing that around your neck!" Josh said.

Dink was looking at a picture of Mel Fisher's boat. "Look, this says it took him almost twenty years to find the treasure!"

"Speaking of food, let's get some lunch," Josh said.

"We weren't talking about food," Ruth Rose said.

"Well, my stomach was," said Josh. "Looking at treasure makes me hungry!"

A few minutes later, the trolley stopped back at the museum.

"What'd you think of all that gold?"

the driver asked them. "Pretty amazing, huh?"

"Did Mel Fisher get to keep everything he found?" Dink asked.

The driver shook his head. "Some had to go to the state of Florida, but he and his investors got rich on the rest."

"What're investors?" Josh asked.

"People who lent Mel Fisher money," said the driver. "Fisher had to borrow a lot to buy equipment and pay his crew. When he struck it rich, he paid his investors back with gold!"

The man grinned in his mirror. "Wish he'd asked *me* to invest!"

A few minutes later the kids said good-bye and hopped off the trolley. They raced home and rushed into Gram Hathaway's kitchen.

"How was your morning?" she asked.

"We rode on the trolley, Gram!"

Ruth Rose said. "The driver was so nice!"

"He dropped us off at the Mel Fisher museum," Dink said.

"And we met two guys who dive for treasure," Josh added. "We went on their boat and saw real gold coins!"

Ruth Rose's grandmother smiled. "I'm glad you got to see some treasure," she said with sparkling eyes. "Now let me tell you about our special company! Their names are Spike and Chip."

Chapter 4

"Gram, how do you know Spike and Chip?" Ruth Rose asked.

"Wash up for lunch, and I'll tell you all about it," her grandmother said.

The kids crowded around the kitchen sink and washed their hands.

"A few weeks ago, Spike and Chip came to my senior center," Ruth Rose's

gram said. She set a plate of sandwiches on the table.

The kids wiped their hands and sat
down.

"They told us all about the treasure
they found!" Gram continued. She
poured lemonade. "Now they're looking
for investors."

"Just like Mel Fisher!" Dink said. He
reached for a tuna sandwich.

"That's right, Dink," Gram said.

Josh heaped three sandwiches onto
his plate. "Are you gonna get rich?" he
asked.

Ruth Rose's grandmother laughed.
"We'll have to wait and see," she said.
"Anyway, we're each thinking about
investing ten thousand dollars!"

"Gram!" Ruth Rose said.

Her grandmother's eyes twinkled. "I
know, it *is* a little scary."

"Boy, I'd do anything to go with

them when they dive for treasure!" Josh said.

"That reminds me," Gram said. She took three presents off the counter. "Merry Christmas!"

"Wow, thanks, Gram!" said Ruth Rose.

"Yeah, thanks!" said Dink and Josh.

"They're all the same," Gram Hathaway said. "That way you won't have to share."

The kids pulled off the paper.

Inside, they each found a book called *Finding Sunken Treasure in Florida.*

The cover showed a boat like the one Mel Fisher had used. Under the boat was a sunken ship. Divers were searching the wreck and bringing up treasure.

"I thought you'd have fun learning about shipwrecks," said Gram, "since I might be investing in one!"

"This is so neat!" Josh said. "Thanks a lot!"

Ruth Rose's grandmother stood up. "You're very welcome. Now I have to get busy. Spike and Chip will be here in an hour! Can you help me set up the living room?"

"Sure," Dink said. "What do you want us to do?"

"I'll need about ten folding chairs. They're in the hall closet. And bring out the three card tables."

The kids arranged the tables and chairs around the living room. Gram Hathaway set out covered plates of cookies on one of the tables.

"Can we stay for the meeting?" Ruth Rose asked.

"Of course!" her grandmother said. "After you read those books, I expect you to ask intelligent questions!"

The kids took their books out to the front porch.

"Look," Josh said. "There's a whole chapter just about Mel Fisher."

Ruth Rose pointed to a map showing sunken ships. "They're all off the coast of Florida," she said. "If each one has treasure on it, think how much that is!"

Josh lay back on the porch and closed his eyes. "I'm staying here when you guys go back home. I'm gonna become a treasure hunter!"

Dink laughed. "*You* find treasure? You couldn't find your shorts this morning, Josh!"

Josh jabbed Dink with his knee. "Call me Captain Josh, please!"

Just then, a car pulled up. Two gray-

haired women climbed out and hurried toward the house.

"I'm going in to help Gram," Ruth Rose said.

"We'll help, too," said Dink. He nudged Josh. "Come on, *Captain* Josh!"

Before they could go inside, a yellow cab stopped out front. Spike and Chip climbed out. Spike was carrying a wooden box. They were both dressed in clean pants, pressed shirts, and sandals.

"Hi!" Josh said as the two men walked up the sidewalk.

Spike and Chip stared at the kids. Finally, Chip waved. "How're you doing? Do you guys live around here?"

Ruth Rose laughed. "No. We're visiting my grandmother. This is her house!"

Spike smiled. "What a small world," he said.

"Can I carry the box in?" Josh asked.

Spike shrugged. "It's pretty heavy."

"I can help," Dink said. They ran down the sidewalk, and Spike handed them the box.

Josh grinned as they lugged the heavy box up the steps. "My fingers feel all tingly!" he said.

Chapter 5

Gram Hathaway's living room was crowded with people. Spike and Chip sat at a small table with the box in front of them. Dink, Josh, and Ruth Rose perched on the stairs.

"Thank you all for coming!" Gram told everyone. Then she smiled at Spike. He stood up.

"Thanks for inviting us," Spike said. "Chip and I have been diving for a few years now. A couple weeks ago, we found a sunken ship."

Chip opened the box. Spike reached in and pulled out a gold cross, about eight inches tall. The gold shone warmly in the sunny room.

Someone said, "Oh, my goodness!" Spike gently laid the cross on the table.

Next he brought out a shiny hunk of silver, about the size of a big bar of soap. Then he spread a handful of gold coins on the table.

"There's a lot more down there," he continued. "We've found chains, silver goblets, even jewelry."

Gram's friends got out of their seats and crowded around Spike and Chip.

"May we touch it?" one woman asked.

Spike laughed. "Can't hurt it,

ma'am. It's been on the bottom of the ocean for almost four hundred years!"

Josh was standing up so he could see. Gram Hathaway's friends were passing around the gold and silver.

"Um, Spike?" Josh said. "How did you get it so clean? Wouldn't it have barnacles and stuff all over it?"

Spike grinned. "Good question," he

said. "First we soak the pieces, then we rub them with regular old vinegar. You'd be surprised how easily it cleans up."

Ruth Rose's hand shot up. "Can I ask a question?"

Spike nodded. "Ask away."

"It took Mel Fisher twenty years to find his sunken ship," said Ruth Rose. "How did you find yours so quickly?"

Spike smiled. "I guess we were just lucky," he said.

"And we had good maps," Chip added.

Spike turned back to the group. "I hope you'll all consider investing with us," he said. "Once we can buy some more equipment, we'll start bringing up some *serious* treasure."

Ruth Rose's grandmother stood up. "Why don't we have refreshments now?" she said.

Everyone began talking and filling small plates with cookies. Ruth Rose went into the kitchen for the lemonade.

Dink and Josh stayed on the stairs, near the table of goodies.

Spike and Chip stepped over to the refreshment table. Dink watched Spike take a few cookies.

"These cookies are loaded with chocolate chips," Spike whispered to his friend.

Dink was about to say something to Spike, but he stopped. He knew he had heard those words before!

Dink closed his eyes and tried to remember the voice he'd overheard in the airport. Dink was positive the man had said "...those cookies are loaded."

Dink was almost sure it had been the same voice!

He looked down for a tattoo, but Spike's pants covered his ankles.

The sandals looked the same. But a lot of people in Florida wore brown leather sandals.

"What's the matter?" Ruth Rose asked Dink. "You look like you smelled something rotten."

Dink stood up. "Come outside," he whispered. "It's important!"

Chapter 6

Josh and Ruth Rose followed Dink through the living room to the porch. They sat on the front steps.

"What's going on?" Josh asked. "I wasn't through with those cookies!"

"Remember the guy I told you about at the airport yesterday?" Dink asked. "Talking on the phone?"

Ruth Rose grinned. "Yeah, the cook you thought was planning a robbery."

Dink turned around and looked through the screen door. "I think it was Spike!"

Josh and Ruth Rose just stared at Dink.

Finally, Josh said, "What are you talking about, Dinkus?"

"I recognized his voice!" Dink said. "The guy at the airport said the same thing, that some old cookies were loaded."

Josh shook his head. "So?"

"Don't you see?" Dink said. "Maybe he meant Gram Hathaway's friends are loaded—loaded with money!"

Suddenly, the door opened, and Gram's friends began coming out. They all seemed excited about investing with Spike and Chip.

Then Spike and Chip came out carrying the box of gold. Gram Hathaway followed them onto the porch.

"Thanks for calling us a cab, Mrs. Hathaway," Spike said. "Do you really think your friends will help us out?"

Gram Hathaway smiled. "I wouldn't be a bit surprised. I'm going to talk to my banker on Monday morning!"

A yellow cab pulled up, and Spike and Chip climbed in with the box. They waved out the window as the cab sped away.

"Wasn't that fun!" Ruth Rose's grandmother said. She stepped back into the house. "There are plenty of goodies left if anyone is hungry!" she called through the screen door.

"Thanks, Gram!" Ruth Rose said.

"She's pretty excited," she added after her grandmother had gone inside.

"I would be, too, if I was gonna get rich," Josh said.

Dink stood up. "Well, I don't think she's gonna get rich," he said. "I think she's gonna get robbed!"

"ROBBED!" Ruth Rose yelled.

"Yeah," Dink said. "Spike and Chip could just take off with your grandmother's money."

"But what about all that gold they just showed us?" Josh asked.

Dink shook his head. "I don't know about that, but I do know what I heard."

"You know what you *thought* you heard," Josh said. "Besides, you don't know it was Spike. You never saw the guy on the phone."

"But I did see his feet!" Dink said. He told Josh and Ruth Rose about the tattoo he'd seen on the man's ankle.

"It's a good thing I'm such an observant young man," Josh said. "I know how we can settle this whole thing."

"How?" Ruth Rose asked.

"By finding out if it really was Spike that Dink heard on the phone."

Dink looked at him. "And how do we do that, oh observant one?"

Josh grinned. "Easy. We get Spike to show us his tattoo!"

Chapter 7

"Good idea," Dink said. "Let's go to the dock."

"Hold on," Ruth Rose said. She opened the screen door, grabbed some towels, and yelled, "GRAM, WE'RE GOING TO THE BEACH!"

Ruth Rose tossed towels to Dink and Josh as they walked down the sidewalk. "What if Spike's still wearing long pants?" she asked.

"Dink will think of something," Josh said. He grinned at Dink. "Right?"

Dink shook his head. "This was your idea. Besides, you're the observant one!"

They thought about it as they walked. When they reached the boat dock, they still hadn't figured out what to do.

"I know," Josh said. "I'll tell him Dink is thinking of getting a tattoo! Then Spike will show us his!"

Dink laughed. "Kids can't get tattoos, Josh," he said.

A few moments later, the kids reached Spike and Chip's boat slip. But the boat wasn't there.

"They're gone!" Ruth Rose said.

"Now what?" Dink asked. "Should we wait till they come back in?"

"Why don't we hang out at the beach for a while?" Josh suggested. "That way, we can have fun and watch for the boat at the same time."

"Okay," Ruth Rose said. "But we can't stay out late. Gram will worry."

"Last one in kisses pelicans!" Josh yelled. He thundered down the dock and leaped onto the beach.

The kids swam, searched for shells, and buried Josh in the sand. By five o'clock, their skin was itchy with sunburn and salt.

"Look, isn't that their boat?" Ruth Rose asked.

A white boat was pulling in at the end of the dock.

"I think it is!" Josh said. "Come on!"

The kids ran back along the dock. They reached the boat as Chip was securing the lines. Spike was behind the wheel, just shutting down the motor.

Both men were wearing T-shirts and jeans. Spike's ankles were covered.

"Did you go diving?" Josh asked.

"We dive every day," Spike said, stepping onto the dock. He patted his stomach. "Right now, I need a couple of burgers. Ready, Chip?"

The kids walked with Spike and Chip to the end of the dock and said good-bye.

"We still didn't see a tattoo," Ruth Rose said as they headed for her grandmother's house.

"No, but I saw something else," Dink said. "They finished painting the name of the boat. It's the *Golden Goose*."

Josh looked at him. "So?"

"The guy at the airport said something about drowning a goose," Dink said. "Maybe that's the goose he was talking about!"

"But what does it mean?" Ruth Rose asked. "Boats don't drown."

Dink shook his head. "I don't know."

A few minutes later, they saw Ruth Rose's grandmother. She was weeding in her front garden.

"Hi, Gram!" Ruth Rose called.

She looked up and waved.

"Tomorrow we go back to the boat and try again," Dink said, keeping his voice low. "You guys with me?"

"What if Spike's still wearing long pants?" Ruth Rose asked.

"Then I put my plan to work," Dink said.

"What plan?" Josh asked.

"I tell him about the tattoo contest," said Dink.

Josh stared at Dink. "What contest?"

"The one I just thought up," Dink said, tapping his head. "I'm gonna hang a poster down by the dock. The poster will announce a tattoo contest. Then I'll tell Spike and Chip about the contest. If Spike has a tattoo on his ankle, he might mention it, or even show it to us."

"Dinkus was in the sun too long," Josh whispered loudly to Ruth Rose.

"I think it's brilliant!" Ruth Rose said. "Come on, I'll ask Gram for paper and markers!"

Chapter 8

Dink jumped out of bed. He shook Josh by the shoulder. "Josh, get up! We're going back to the dock!"

Josh opened one eye. "Time izzit?" he asked sleepily.

Dink glanced at the clock next to his bed. "Almost eight. Hurry up!"

Dink dressed in shorts and a T-shirt.

He washed, brushed his hair, and grabbed the poster he'd drawn the night before.

"Come on, Josh!" he said, hurrying downstairs.

Ruth Rose was sitting at the table, spreading peanut butter on a bagel.

"Gram's out for her morning swim," she said. She pushed the plate of bagels toward Dink. "Where's Josh?"

Dink sat down and reached for the strawberry jam. "Still waking up," he said.

Dink unrolled the poster as Josh stumbled into the kitchen. His red hair was sticking straight up. "This plan had better work," he said. "I was dreaming I was King Midas. Only everything I touched turned to chocolate!"

Josh got a bagel and read Dink's poster through sleepy eyes. At the bottom Dink had drawn a man's arm with

COME ONE, COME ALL!

TATTOO CONTEST
ON THE PIER
Sunday night at 8:00

CASH PRIZES FOR THE
MOST CREATIVE TATTOOS!

a tattoo of an owl.

"What happens when a bunch of people with tattoos show up, and there's no contest?" Josh asked.

Dink shrugged. "We have to find out if Spike has that tattoo on his ankle. Can you think of another way?"

Josh just shrugged.

"All right, then. Let's get going," Dink said.

They each grabbed an apple and headed for the dock. Dink carried the poster and four thumbtacks.

Even this early, people were strolling along the concrete pier. Dink tacked the poster to a light pole.

"Okay, now let's go find Spike and Chip," he said. They hurried to the dock.

A few people were on their boats, drinking coffee and enjoying the morning sun. The *Golden Goose* was tied at its slip.

Not a sound came from the boat.

"Think they're still asleep?" Josh asked.

Dink shrugged. "I don't hear any snoring."

Ruth Rose peered through one of

the round cabin windows. "Nobody's down there," she said.

"Look, the door's open," Josh said. "They must be here."

Dink stepped onto the boat deck and knocked on the wood. "Hello?" he called. "Anyone home?"

Dink hopped back onto the dock. "Maybe they went out for breakfast," he said. "Let's wait."

The kids sat in the sun. A pelican waddled along the dock, stopping at each of the boats. A woman tossed him some bread.

Josh pulled his book out and began reading.

"Listen to this," he said. "'No matter how long it has been on the bottom of the ocean, gold stays shiny. But silver requires several days in a special chemical solution before it looks shiny again.'"

Josh looked up. "Yesterday, Spike told everyone they cleaned the gold and silver with vinegar!"

The kids looked at each other.

Dink got up and stepped aboard the *Golden Goose.* He walked around the deck, looking at everything and peeking into corners.

He stopped near an oxygen tank propped against a bench, then came back to the dock.

"That tank's empty," he told Josh and Ruth Rose.

"How do you know?" Josh asked.

"There's a round window with a dial," Dink said. "The little arrow is pointing to E."

"So maybe they used up all the oxygen and haven't filled it up yet."

"Maybe," Dink said. "But I don't see any other diving equipment."

Ruth Rose stepped closer to the

deck. "Maybe they keep it down below," she said. She looked at the guys. "I say we check it out."

"Me too," Dink said.

Josh glanced back toward the pier. "What if they come back and catch us snooping?" he said.

"We'll tell them my grandmother sent us," Ruth Rose said. "I'll say she wants to ask them more questions."

"I think they hang pirates," Josh said.

"Josh, just looking on someone's boat doesn't make us pirates," Ruth Rose said. "If they're trying to cheat my grandmother, I'm gonna find out! Come on, we won't touch anything, we'll just look around."

She hopped aboard the boat and scooted down the cabin stairs. Josh and Dink followed.

The three stood in the middle of the

small cabin. "What a smell!" Ruth Rose said.

"They aren't very neat, are they?" Josh said. The beds were unmade, and the tiny kitchen was a jumble of dirty dishes and glasses. The small eating table was covered with sticky-looking stains.

Dink glanced into a few dark corners. "I still don't see—"

"Shh! I heard something!" Ruth Rose said. She pointed above their heads. Suddenly, they all heard footsteps.

The kids looked at each other, wide-eyed.

Josh's face was white.

Dink looked around the small cabin, then rushed toward a narrow door in the back.

He yanked the door open and motioned for Josh and Ruth Rose to follow.

Chapter 9

The kids found themselves crammed in the boat's tiny bathroom.

There was no room to sit or turn around. The kids just stood and stared at each other.

Suddenly, they heard heavy feet thunder down the cabin stairs. They held their breath.

They heard a small thump, then a bigger one. Then the feet were walking again, this time going up the stairs.

The small room got hot fast. Sweat ran into Dink's eyes. He could barely breathe.

They waited, but heard no more noises.

"I smell scrambled eggs!" Josh whispered into Dink's ear.

Dink rolled his eyes.

"Well, I do!" said Josh.

Dink waited a few more minutes, then opened the door a crack. Cool air rushed into the bathroom.

Dink quickly looked around the cabin. He could hear the men talking up above. He gently pulled the door shut.

"They're up on deck," he said. "We can't stay in this bathroom. If one of them wants to use it, we're sunk!"

"Why don't we just leave?" Josh asked.

"How do we explain why we're hiding in their boat?" Ruth Rose said. "It's too late!"

Dink slipped out of the bathroom and saw a trapdoor in the floor.

Kneeling, Dink pulled the trapdoor open. Josh and Ruth Rose tiptoed out of the bathroom.

Suddenly, the kids heard a roar. Then Dink felt the boat begin to move—backward!

"They're taking the boat out!" he whispered. "Come on, down here!"

The kids scampered down into the boat's hold. Dink lowered the door over their heads. Except for a crack of light around the trapdoor, they were in darkness.

"This place stinks like rotten fish!" Josh said.

"Now what?" Ruth Rose said.

"I don't know," Dink answered. He thought for a minute.

"They must be going out to the dive site," he said. "We'll have to hide till they decide to go back to the dock."

"But that could be all day!" Josh said.

The kids squirmed around, trying to get comfortable.

Dink put his eye up to the crack and saw the underside of the table. To the right, he could just make out the bottom stair leading up to the deck.

"Ouch!" Josh said suddenly. "I think I sat on an anchor!"

"And I scraped my knee on a cinder block!" Ruth Rose said.

Dink moved his hands around the sloping wooden floor. His fingers felt hard, scratchy surfaces. More cinder blocks, a bunch of them.

Then he touched something squishy.

"Guys, I found some life vests," Dink whispered. "Put 'em on!"

The kids struggled into the vests. Dink kept his eye on the crack. He wanted to know if Spike or Chip came down into the cabin.

"Whose idea was it to get on this boat?" Josh said. "I feel like a prisoner!"

"You wanted to go out on a dive," Dink said. "You got your wish!"

"Yeah," Josh said. "But not trapped in some smelly dungeon!"

Dink saw a movement through the crack. A pair of bare feet were backing down the stairs!

"Shh!" he said. "They're coming down to the cabin!"

They heard footsteps, then voices. Shapes moved back and forth across the trapdoor.

"This place is a pigpen," one of the men said. Dink recognized Spike's voice.

"Why bother to clean it?" Chip answered. He giggled. "It'll get real clean in a little while."

Dink heard something scrape, then a thump right over his head.

Through the crack, he saw skinny wooden legs. A stool or chair had been dragged up to the small table.

"We got any juice?" Spike asked.

"I doubt it," Chip answered. "I think there's milk."

"They're eating breakfast!" Josh hissed into Dink's ear. "I told you I smelled eggs!"

Then somebody sat down at the table. Dink could see one person's leg from the knee down.

The leg was hairy and tanned.

Suddenly, Dink gasped. Just inches
from his eye, he saw a tattoo.

It was an eagle's head.

Chapter 10

Spike *was* the man he'd overheard at the airport!

Suddenly, Chip was talking. "Ya know," he said, "I'm gonna miss this old tub when it's gone."

"Not me," Spike answered. "When we get the dough from the old folks, I'm buying the hottest car in Florida.

I'm sick of living like a sardine!"

"So when do you want to do it?" Chip asked.

"Soon as I finish eating," Spike said. "I'll even let you have the pleasure of using the ax."

Dink heard Chip laugh. "With all those cinder blocks we brought aboard, the *Goose* will go down in ten seconds!"

"Yeah, it should," Spike said. "Don't forget the box. We don't want that to sink, too!"

Dink felt Josh grab his arm and squeeze. On his other side, Ruth Rose let out a small gasp.

Spike and Chip were planning to sink the *Golden Goose!*

"Don't worry," Chip was saying. "I already put the gold in the dinghy."

A chair scraped, and the tattooed ankle disappeared from Dink's sight.

"After we drown the *Goose,* we'll

take the dinghy back to town," Spike said. "We'll lie low till we get the money from the old folks."

He laughed. "Then we disappear."

Dink felt his stomach sink. He heard more thumps and footsteps.

"Make sure you don't leave anything aboard with your name on it," Spike said. "Paper floats, you know."

"Don't worry," Chip said. "Where's the ax?"

The voices faded away.

"Did you hear that?" Josh asked. "They're gonna sink this thing!"

"Shh!" Dink hissed. Suddenly, the kids heard loud smashing noises, one after the other.

Dink gulped. It was an ax striking wood!

Then he heard a thump and footsteps running up the cabin stairs.

Suddenly, he heard a new sound—

the gurgle of water flooding into the boat!

"Now!" Dink said. He shoved the trapdoor open and scrambled out. Josh and Ruth Rose were right behind him.

They stepped into salt water.

"Look!" Ruth Rose pointed to a hole in the side of the cabin. Water was rushing in.

"What are we gonna do?" Josh asked.

Dink raced up the stairs and peeked. He saw Spike and Chip tearing across the water in the dinghy.

"They took off!" Dink said. "Come on!"

The kids ran up the stairs and sprinted toward the rear of the boat.

Josh looked down into the water. "Now what do we do?" he squeaked.

"WE JUMP!" Ruth Rose yelled.

And they did.

Chapter 11

Dink felt the water rush over his head. Some got in his mouth before he remembered to shut it. His eyes stung from the salt.

Then his life vest shot him to the surface. He was floating.

Josh and Ruth Rose were bobbing nearby in their orange life vests.

"You guys okay?" Dink asked.

"Look!" Josh said, pointing at something over Dink's shoulder.

Dink spun around in the water.

The *Golden Goose* lay on its side. A few seconds later, it went under.

The kids heard a loud WHOOSH! as the boat disappeared.

"We got off just in time!" Josh said.

"Let's swim," Dink said. "Spike and Chip might decide to come back to make sure the boat sank!"

"Swim where?" Josh asked. "I can't even see land!"

"But I see some boats," Ruth Rose said, pointing one wet arm. "See those things sticking up out of the water?"

Josh began splashing his arms. "I think those are shark fins!" he yelled.

Ruth Rose laughed. "Sharks don't have white sails, Josh."

The kids began swimming toward

the boats. Suddenly, Dink heard a roar.

He whipped his head around, expecting to see Spike and Chip bearing down on them. Instead, he saw a large white boat. On the side, in black letters, he read COAST GUARD.

The boat zoomed up, then slowed.

The kids bounced in the waves like corks.

"What the heck are you kids doing!" a voice boomed from the boat.

Dink saw a man in a white uniform standing on the deck. He was holding a bullhorn and glaring down at them.

Dink tried to yell, but a wave filled his mouth with water.

Another man threw three round life preservers into the water. "Hang on to those!" the man in white bellowed.

The rings splashed into the water only a few feet away.

Seconds later, Dink, Josh, and Ruth Rose were hauled onto the boat's deck.

The kids huddled together. A group of men stood staring at them.

The sun was warm, but Dink couldn't stop shaking.

One of the men draped blankets around their shoulders.

"Well?" the uniformed man said. "I'm waiting."

He stared at the kids with a strange expression on his face. "You do speak English, I hope."

Josh grinned. "Yeah. Do you guys have anything to eat? I'm starving!"

The men laughed.

The man holding the bullhorn grinned. "Okay, kids, first you tell us why you were swimming to Cuba," he said, "then we feed you!"

"Awesome!" Josh said as burst after burst of fireworks went off in the sky. It was ten o'clock on New Year's Eve, two days after they'd been rescued by the Coast Guard boat.

The kids were lying on the lawn in Gram's backyard. They had just finished a lobster dinner, and their stomachs were full.

Gram came out carrying a tray. "Who has room for chocolate ice cream?" she asked.

Dink groaned. "If I eat one more thing, I'll bust wide open!"

Josh sat up. "I'll have some!" he said.

Gram set the tray on the blanket. "Help yourself," she said, joining the kids.

"That was a super meal, Gram," Ruth Rose said.

"My pleasure!" Gram said. "You kids are heroes! Thanks to you, the police were able to catch Spike and Chip. We almost lost a lot of money!"

"Well, Dinkus," Josh said, "you were right. It was Spike on the phone at the airport, and he did say, 'take the dough!'"

Gram Hathaway squeezed Dink's hand. "You saved the day!" she said.

Dink blushed. "Well, you guys helped, too," he said. "If it hadn't been for Ruth Rose, we wouldn't have been on the *Golden Goose* when those two guys came back. They'd have sunk the boat *and* gotten away with the money."

"And Josh figured out they were lying about how to clean gold and silver," Ruth Rose said. "I never even saw that in my book."

Gram Hathaway smiled. "I know three children who are going to get a reward," she said.

"A reward?" Josh said. "For what?"

"The gold and silver Spike and Chip showed us was stolen from a museum in Miami," Gram said. "The museum was offering a reward, and it goes to you three!"

"Awesome—how much?" Josh said.

Ruth Rose laughed. "Don't be greedy, Joshua."

Josh slurped up the last of his ice cream. "I'm not greedy," he said. "I just like money!"

Suddenly, a huge mushroom of fireworks went off over their heads. Red, blue, and green sprays of light cascaded toward the earth.

"Make a wish, everyone!" Gram said.

"I wish I had more ice cream," Josh said.

"I wish I had my own computer," Ruth Rose said.

"I wish we could stay here longer," Dink said. "Our vacation went by so fast!"

Gram Hathaway gave Dink a kiss on the cheek. "Your wish is granted," she said. "You're all invited back this summer!"